Three Strikes and You're Out

Modern Curriculum Press
BEGINNING
TO
READ
Series

Three Strikes and You're Out

Valjean McLenighan

Illustrated by Laurie Hamilton

MODERN CURRICULUM PRESS
Pearson Learning Group

ISBN: 0-8136-5585-4
Printed in the United States of America

10 11 12 13 14 15 16 17   06 05 04 03 02

1-800-321-3106
www.pearsonlearning.com

Once there was a poor woman.
Things were hard for her and her boy.

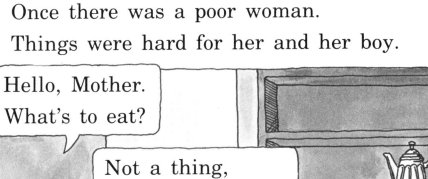

Hello, Mother.
What's to eat?

Not a thing,
I am sorry to say.

So off went the boy to see his aunt.

Mother and I have nothing to eat. Can you help us out?

I have just the thing. Take this bird.

Thanks. Mother makes a good chicken soup.

Soup! Not on your life! This is not just any old bird. Watch this.

Now go right
home. Watch
that chicken.
Don't tell what
she can do.

9

The boy and his chicken came to an inn.

Well, the boy got his room.

But the man knew something was up.

That night he found out what it was.

As soon as the boy went to sleep,
the man changed chickens.

The next morning . . .

The boy went to the man.
It did not do any good.

The boy went back to his aunt.
He told all.

He even called me a clown.

Don't be blue.
You get three strikes
before you're out.

Now take this cloth.

Thanks.
It will
make some
nice shirts.

15

Shirts! Not on your life!
This is not just any
old cloth. Put it down.
Tell it you want
to eat. Then watch
what happens.

16

The boy did as his aunt said.
At once he had all he could eat.

Now take that cloth and go right home. Don't tell what it can do.

If only the boy had done just that! But no. He stopped at the inn.

Give me a room for my cloth and me.

Well, the man knew something was up.
That night he found out what it was.

As soon as the boy went to sleep,
the man changed cloths.

The next morning . . .

The boy did not even stop at the inn.
He went right back to his aunt.

These things happen. You get
three strikes before you're out.
And speaking of strikes —

I have just the thing for you. Take this walking stick. I will tell you what to do.

Soon the boy was back at the inn.

Good to see you again.
Nice stick you have there.

The man could not wait to get that stick.
He did not even care what it could do.
He was greedy. That is what did him in.

Late that night, he went to the boy's room.
This time, the boy was ready.

Strike one!

27

Strike two!

Ow! Ow! Two strikes are plenty.
I will give you back your bird
and cloth. Take them and that
stick and go home. Please.

The boy and his mother were no longer poor. Every Sunday they gave a party. People came from all over.

There was always plenty to eat. Those
who needed money could ask the chicken.
And the stick took care
of the greedy people.

Valjean McLenighan, is a writer, editor, and producer.

Three Strikes and You're Out uses the 161 words listed.

a	did	had	make(s)
about	do(n't)	happens	man
again	done	hard	me
all	down	have	money
always		he	morning
am	eat	heard	Mother
an	even	hello	my
and	ever	help	
any	every	her	next
as		here	nice
ask	for	him	night
at	found	his	no
aunt	from	home	not
		how	nothing
back	gave		now
be(ing)	get	I	
before	give(s)	if	of
bird	go(ing)	in	off
blue	good	inn	oh
boy	got	is	old
but	greedy	it	on
			once
called		just	only
came			out
can		knew	over
care			ow
changed		last	
chicken(s)		late	
cloth(s)		life	
clown		longer	
could		lunch	

party	take	wait
pay	tell	walking
people	thanks	was
pets	that	watch
please	the	well
plenty	them	went
poor	then	were
put	there	what('s)
	these	when
ready	they	who
right	thing(s)	will
room	this	with
	those	woman
said	three	
see	time	you('re)
she	to	your
shirts	told	
sleep	two	
so		
some	up	
something	us	
soon		
sorry		
soup		
speaking		
stays		
stick		
stop(ped)		
strike(s)		
Sunday		